FOX 8

RANDOM HOUSE
NEW YORK

FOX 8

~

A Story

~

GEORGE SAUNDERS

Illustrations by Chelsea Cardinal

Published in the United States by Random House, an imprint and division of Penguin Random House LLC, New York.

RANDOM HOUSE and the HOUSE colophon are registered trademarks of Penguin Random House LLC.

Originally published as an ebook in the United States by Random House, an imprint and division of Penguin Random House LLC, in 2013.

Hardback ISBN 978-1-9848-1802-7
Ebook ISBN 978-0-8129-9532-9

Printed in the United States of America
on acid-free paper

randomhousebooks.com

2 4 6 8 9 7 5 3 1

FIRST HARDCOVER EDITION

Illustrations by Chelsea Cardinal

FOX 8

Deer Reeder:

First may I say, sorry for any werds I spel rong. Because I am a fox! So don't rite or spel perfect. But here is how I lerned to rite and spel as gud as I do!

One day, walking neer one of your Yuman houses, smelling all the interest with snout, I herd, from inside, the most amazing sound. Turns out, what that sound is, was: the Yuman voice, making werds. They sounded grate! They sounded like pretty music! I listened to those music werds until the sun went down, when all of the suden I woslike: Fox 8, crazy nut, when sun goes down, werld goes dark, skedaddle home, or else there can be danjer!

But I was fast and nated by those music

werds, and desired to understand them total lee.

So came bak nite upon nite, seeted upon that window, trying to lern. And in time, so many werds came threw my ears and into my brane, that, if I thought upon them, cud understand Yuman prety gud, if I heer it!

What that lady in that house was saying, was: Storys, to her pups, with "luv." When done, she wud dowse the lite, causing dark. Then, due to feeling "luv," wud bend down, putting snout and lips to the heds of her pups, which was called: "gudnite kiss." Which I got a kik out of that! Because that is also how we show our luv for our pups, as Foxes! It made me feel gud, like Yumans cud feel luv and show luv. In other werds, hope full for the future of Erth!

But one nite I herd something that made me think twise about Yumans.

And I still am.

What I herd was a Story, but a fawlse and even meen one. In that story was a Fox. But guess what the Fox was? Sly! Yes, true lee! He trikked a Chiken! He lerd this plump Chiken away from its henhowse, claming there is some feed in a stump. We do not trik Chikens! We are very open and honest with Chikens! With Chikens, we have a Super Fare Deel, which is: they make the egs, we take the egs, they make more egs. And sometimes may even eat a live Chiken, shud that Chiken consent to be eaten by us, threw faling to run away upon are approche, after she has been looking for feed in a stump.

Not Sly at all.

Very strate forword.

That Story was also fawlse due to the mane Chiken is whering glases. Which, Chikens that

I know of? Do not where glases. I do not think this is because all Chikens see grate. I think it is because Chikens do not even know when they don't see grate, due to, altho I have the highest respek for Chikens, luvving their egs, they are perchanse not the britest.

But Chikens whering glases was not the only fawlse Story I herd.

Like I herd Storys about Bares, in which Bares are always sleeping and nise and luvving. Beleev me, as someone offen chased by Bares, never was a Bare chasing me (1) asleep or (2) nise and (3) luvving. You shud heer the many not-nise things a Bare is saying, in Bare, as he is chasing you, as lukily you slide into your Den just in the nack of time and try not to start crying in front of your other Foxes.

And in terms of Owls, Owls are wise? Don't make me laff! Once a Owl nipped Fox 6 kwite crool on his nek just because Fox 6 was saying a frend lee greeting to the baby Owls with his snout!

For a long time, no one but me knew I knew Yuman. Then one day, as faith will have it, I am walking threw the wuds with Fox 7, a gud pal, when all of the suden a branch drops down on us from upon hi.

And I woslike: O wow.

But said not in Fox, but in Yuman.

Fox 7 was so shokked he just sat with haunch on ground and tung lolling out, along with the wide eyes of being complete lee as-tonish.

To which I said: Correct, what I just now spoke, was Yuman, dude.

And he woslike: That is pretty gud, Fox 8.

To which I woslike, in Yuman, to perhaps show off slite: It is super gud, no dowt, Fox 7.

And he woslike: We must tell our Grate Leeder. This is so—

To which, in Fox, I woslike: I know, rite?

So we went to our Grate Leeder, Fox 28, and I spoke him some Yuman.

When I had spoken my Yuman, Grate Leeder turned his hed sidewise the way us Foxes do when feeling quizmical or a noise is hi, and said: Fox 8, how did you akomplish this?

I woslike: By studying their speech patterns every nite without fale.

He woslike: Perhaps you wud be gud enough to use your new skil to help the Groop?

I was kwite flatered by this show of respek from Grate Leeder, famus among us for wize consel, plus always leeding us grate.

I woslike: Hapy to help.

Grate Leeder woslike: Folow me, Fox 8.

Which I did, shooting Fox 7 a prowd look of: Dude, chek me out.

Soon we are standing before a sine, and upon that sine are some Yuman letters like the ones I had been lerning. And thanks to my studies, I cud reed it. (Lukily, I had lerned their alphobet, by skwinting my eyes, threw that window, at their buks.)

What those werds said, is: Coming soon, FoxViewCommons.

I red them to Grate Leeder, who, bak in are Den, said them alowd to the Groop.

Those werds caused many suden questions in all our branes. Such as: What is a FoxView-Commons? Wud it chase us? Wud it eat us?

Terns out, it cud not eat us. It cud not chase us. But what it cud do, was even werse.

Because soon here came Truks, smoking wile tooting! They dug up our Primary Forest!

They tore out our Leaning Tree! They rekked our shady drinking spot, and made total lee flat the highest plase of which we know, from where we can see all of curashun if it is not raning!

Whoa was us.

As far as we cud see, it is just flat, no trees. Upon troting to our River, we found it rekked due to so much suden dirt floting in. Also rekked were are Fish who, not even swoping a single flipper, just glansed up blank at us, like: Wow, we do not even get what just hapened.

Wile trying to explane it was Truks that hapened, we lerned one reason they cud not swope a flipper is, they are ded! Plus not only are our Fish ded, but all the things we luv to eat, such as Bugs, such as fat slow Mise, are total lee gone! We serched all day, snouts low. But not one snak.

Soon sevral of our Extreme Lee Old Foxes become sik, and ded, because: no fud. These ded frends were: Fox 24, Fox 10, and Fox 111.

Gud Foxes all.

One leson I lerned during my nites at that Yuman window was: a gud riter will make the reeder feel as bad as the Yuman does in there Story. Like the riter will make you feel as bad as Sinderela. You will feel sad you cannot go to the danse. And mad you have to sweep. You will feel like biting Stepmother on her Gown. Or, if you are Penokio, you will feel like: I wud rather not be made of wud. I wud rather be made of skin, so my father Jipeta will stop hitting me with a hamer. And so farth.

If you want to feel as bad as we Foxes are feeling at this time: (1) bare lee eat for weeks, (2) note that many frends, including you, are getting skinyer every day, and (3) watch sevral of your beluvved frends get so skiny they die.

At this time, Grate Leeder grew kwite sad. It was like he grew too sad to leed. And wud sit for hours staring into spase. It woslike Grate Leeder blamed himself that we had lost are Forest in which we had always lived since time in memorial. But we did not feel it was his fawlt. It hapened so fast, who cud have been grate enough to stop it? (I for sure did not know how to stop it. Once I snuk into the bak of a Truk and stole there hamer with my mouth. I know it is not gud to steel but I was so mad! But me steeling that hamer did not even slow them down. They must have had other hamers?)

Finally some of us went to Grate Leeder and are like: Grate Leeder, let us go farth and find some fud, plus a better plase to live.

But he just did this mone, and woslike: No,

no, it is too danjerus. Everyone stay rite here where I can see you.

And once again plased hed between paws.

Week upon week the Truks kep werking. These Yumans sure cud werk. They werked and werked until soon a hole forest is gone. How did they do it?

With there hands, plus Truks.

Terns out, what they were making is: sevral big wite boxes, with, written upon them, mistery werds. Upon my reeding of these werds, my felow Foxes looked at me all quizmical, like: Fox 8, tell us, what is Bon-Ton, what is Compu-Fun, what is Hooters, what is Kookies-N-Cream?

But I cud not say, those werds never being herd by me at my Story window.

FoxViewCommons seemed to be a plase Yumans came to put there Kars. They wud go into the wite boxes and wate there until there Kars were redy to go home? Sometimes I wud go up to a Kar, inside of which there is a Dog, and, due to speeking decent Dog, wud be like:

How's it going? To which the Dog wud either look blank at me, as if I was not even speeking Dog, or fling themself around inside there Kar, as if they wud like to brake out and do damage to me, a Fox!

But finally one Dog does answer, going: Prety gud, how about you? It is reely hot in here.

And I woslike: Frend, what is this plase?

He woslike: Par King.

I woslike: What is it for?

At which point he took a paws to lik his but. Wile I polite lee wated.

Finally he woslike: The Mawl.

I woslike: But what is the purpose of the Mawl?

By this time, however, he is asleep. With legs running, yet stil traped in that Kar, probly dreeming he is a Fox, with Fox lee freedom, and less pudgee.

But he was rite: it was Par King, it was the Mawl. Yumans wud go: You kids stop fiting, we're at the Mawl, kwit, kwit it, if you don't stop fiting how wud you like it if we just skip the Mawl and you can get rite to your aljuh-bruh, Kerk? Or, speeking into a small box, a Yuman mite go, I have to run, Jeenie, I'm just now Par King at the Mawl! Or one Yuman slaps the but of a sekond, and the slapt one leens in, kwite fond, going, Elyut, you kil me. Or a lady drops her purse and bends to retreev her guds, when sudden lee her hat blows away, at which

time, speeking a bad werd, she looks redy to sit and cry, own lee a nise man appeers, and rases off in kwest of her hat, tho he has a slite limp.

Yumans!

Always intresting.

One day I am krowching at the edge of Par King, gazing over at the Mawl, when out comes a pare of Yumans.

One woslike: OK, I will meet you at the Fud Cort when you are done with your lip waks.

And the other woslike: If you are late I will total lee kill you, Meggen.

And the other woslike: Don't worry, I'll find you. You'll be the one with the way red lip.

Then they laffed.

That frase of "Fud Cort" prikked up my ears but gud.

Mite there be fud in a Fud Cort?

There mite, I felt.

Here I shud say, all my life, I have had kwite curative day-dreems. They wud just come upon me. And I wud enjoy them.

With some favrits being:

Some Yumans heer me speeking Yuman so gud they give me some Chiken, and I sit rite at there Table. And they go: How is it being a Fox?

And I go: Fine.

And they go: Foxes are our favrit Animal.

And I go: Thanks.

And they go: Why o why were we so stupid as to choose Dogs for our mane Pets?

And I go: I reely don't know.

Or: Some Bares are chasing me. I stop and, holding one paw aleft, give them a speech about being nise, and they are like: Maybe this is weerd to ask, but cud you, a Fox, be our Grate Leeder, and teech us to be nise and not walk funy? And I go: Sure. And they applawd with their paws. But awkword. So I teech them to clap gud and they look at me with luv.

Or: Some Berds fly around my hed, going: What a prety Fox, we have flown everywhere in this werld and never seen one pretier! And one Berd goes: And smart too. And the others churp there agreement.

Now, krowching neer Par King, I had a curative day-dreem, about Fud Cort, which was: Go in, get some fud. Why not? How hard cud it be? If there is fud, it shud be fud for all, rite?

That nite, at Groop Meeting, I brot farth my plan.

But sad lee, my somewhat reputashun as a dreemer preseded me.

And not in a gud way.

Grate Leeder woslike: What is Fud Cort anyway? Sounds danjerus.

I woslike: Yumans are nise, they are cul.

And Fox 41 woslike, all snoty: O rite! Very funy! I'm sure we are going to trust the same Fox who once clamed he went to Collage with some Baby!

Fox 41 bringing up that Baby was so not cul.

Once, long ago, at that Story window, I daydreemed those Yumans invited me in and let me hold there Baby. And that Baby luvved me so much, we soon jerneyed to Collage together, whering are little Collage Hats! It was grate! At Collage we lerned such Yuman skils as Werking Machines, and How to Play a Violin Complete Lee Screechy.

But when I came home and told my Foxes about going to Collage with that Baby, they did not beleev me. To proov it, I desided to show them my Collage Hat.

Which was when I remembered I had day-dreemed the hole thing.

The only Collage Hat I had was in my brane! Tray embarasing.

So that is why, in Groop Meeting, Grate Leeder woslike: No, Fox 8. No Mawl. Gud input tho.

I terned to my other Foxes and woslike: Guys, pleese suport me on this.

But fownd the eyes of my other Foxes lolling up at the seeling.

Fox 4 woslike: No ofense, Fox 8? Your ideas are not super praktikal.

Dreem, dreem, dreem, said Fox 11.

Fox 41 woslike: Fox 8, does this honestly never get old for you?

Grate Leeder woslike: I have spoken.

And something in me woslike: Grate Leeder, bla.

I still luvved him but it woslike he was not being all that Grate. Or even a Leeder. I meen no disrespek. It was just a strong feeling in my hart that it was no gud for Foxes to give up and just be ded on perpose.

All that nite I cud not sleep for beens. But just lay awake, looking sad lee around at all my sleeping Foxes. And woslike, in my brane: Frends, you do not look so gud. The hare of your cotes is manjee. You are neerly all eyes, due to: super hungry. Your sides are like heeving in your sleep. Deer Foxes! You have known me sinse, as a Pup, I tried to bite my own face in our Rivver. You knew me bak when, day-dreeming, I stepped in Poop of Wolf and brot it bak inside the Den, causing everyone to rinkle their snouts, going like: Fox 8, jeez, how cud you not smell Poop of Wolf when it is rite on your own dang paw? But you forgave me, and

when I had got most of the Poop off, by rubing against a tree, even helped me lik myself all the way gud.

And sinse I luv you, shud I not do my best to save you?

Hense I desided to go alone.

And next morning set off for the Mawl.

You may have herd the Yuman frase, What are frends for? Well, I will tell you. Frends are for, when your hole Groop terns its baks on you, here comes your frend, Fox 7, of who I spoke of erlyer, as being the first Fox I ever spoke Yuman to, troting up beside you.

He woslike: I'll go with you, Fox 8.

I woslike: Dude.

He gave this small shrug, like: No big deel.

We troted awile in gud cheer. Soon here was the Mawl. Cud we kros Par King? We cud. And did.

Here is how you do it:

Take a deep breth. Look left and look rite, very vigrus. Careful, careful.

Go. Go go go! Do not even paws.

FoxViewCommons is now bowncing, because you are galupping so fast.

A Kar almost gets you! Do a panic-yip. Stop. Take a slite brake under another Kar. Try to go. Too bad, you can't. Too skared! Do a miner worry-yip.

Go!

Paws!

Look again, look again. Go. Stop! Look again.

Just reely buk it!

You made it!

And are not ded.

But now there was a problem we had not mulled, which is: a Dore. Dores being a problem for Foxes, due to being hevy, plus there handels may be hi.

But luk was with us.

Just then, a very Yung Yuman, a meer Todler, todled past with a smile of possibly thinking we are Dogs. There in her hand, we noted: some fud! It looked gud and smelled grate. It is a Bun! All of the suden, we desided to enter into a Fare Deel with her, whereby we wud share her Bun, by us taking it.

But then, quik as the wink, she is intaken into the Mawl, with one hand in the hand of her Mother and, in the other hand, our Bun! And before we knew it, we too, lerd by her fud, had been intaken into FoxViewCommons, rite threw their Dore!

There is a hi music sound. The ground is like glas. Or ise.

And o my frends, the things we saw!

We saw the Gap! We saw Eye Openers! We saw a Pet Store, with captured Kats! We saw a

small River that, tho flowing, did not smell rite. We saw some Fake Rox. We saw Trees. Reel Trees, inside FoxViewCommons! It made us want to dig a Den! We saw a groop of Yung Yumans, waring brite close and dansing fast, and some Old Yumans we think are there mothers, hopping about kwite eksited, yeling advise, such as, Pik it up, Kristal! Or Smile, Kara, why look so sad wile dansing, babe? We saw a round thing which had Fake Horses upon it, on which they are enslaved and made to go circular, as Yung Yumans enjoy it by being plased on bak of them. I was left to wonder: Why wud Old Yumans enjoy putting Yung Yumans on Fake Horses? It was a total mistery. And remanes so. It is as if an Old Fox enjoys putting his Yung Fox on a Fake Deer. I for one wud not enjoy that. Altho it might be funy at first.

Yumans wud walk by and go: Hey, look, Foxes. And drop a bit of fud at us. Soon we had karmel korn, sevral parshul biskits, plus a pare so fresh it did not even stink.

I woslike: This must be Fud Cort.

Fox 7 woslike: I gess so.

We were so happy we sat between those Fake Rox, speeking dreemy lee of our future, such as: We wud get some pants and glases. We wud ride in a Kar, plasing a coffee on are breefcase. We wud make such gud frends with the Yumans, they wud cut a Fox Dore in there Mawl.

Never had Yumans seemed so cul. We were sarounded by splender no Fox cud curate. Hense were fild with respek. Cud a Fox do this? Bild a Mawl? Fat chanse! The best we can do is dig are Dens.

Then it was time to go home.

For we now had fud sufishent to save the lifes of our frends.

Holding that fud in are mowths, we troted bak threw FoxViewCommons, heds held hi, having such a feeling of pride, being probly the first Foxes or even Animals ever inside Fox-ViewCommons, except for those captured Kats.

Out we went.

Here again was the Sun! Here again Clowds! I cud not wate to see Fox 41, and go: Hi, Fox 41, perfeshunal turd, care for some fud?

But upon reaching the edge of Par King, guess what we did not find?

Fox 41.

Or are other Foxes.

Or are Den.

It woslike we had gone out a hole difrent Dore than we had gone in threw.

Now, one thing I lerned from Storys is, when something big is about to okur, a riter will go: Then it hapened!

This tells the reeder: Get Reddy.

Here I go:

Then it hapened!

There at the edj of Par King was a teem of two Yumans doing some digging. One woslike: Holy krap, Foxes! As if he had never seen a Fox before. My feeling was: Yes, yes, we are Foxes, hello frends, we have just seen the wunder that is your Mawl, we congradulate you! We glampsed your fake River, obserbed your cute yung ones dansing, gladly acsepted your generus gift of Fud. You are so nise! What a grate day for the Fox/Yuman conection!

Then that first Yuman, kwite huje, took off a blue hat he was wearing. And I woslike, in my brane: It must be a form of saloot? So did a Fox saloot back, which is: reach out with front legs, bow, yawn. Only then, running toward us in a startling maner, he threw that hat at us! From the sound it made upon not hitting us, but only Par King, I saw it must be made of rok. I gave Fox 7 a glanse, like: What

did we do rong? Then the other Yuman, kwite small, ran at us, and threw his hat, and o my frends, what hapened next is hard to rite. Because that hat wonked Fox 7 skware in his face! And sudenly his nees go week, and he gives me one last fond look, and drops over on his side, with blud trikling out his snout! I breefly tried to revive him, by sniffing. But here comes the huje and the small Yuman, running as if in viktree, making a noise that made my hare stand on my nek, and what cud I do but flee?

Glansing bak wile troting, I saw the huje and small Yuman doing such things to Fox 7 as: further hits with their hats, and kiks and stomps, wile making adishunal noises I had never herd a Yuman make, as if this is fun, as if this is funy, as if they are prowd of what they are akomplishing! Reeching a dirt klod big as me, I lay behind it, panting wile shaking.

Which is when I saw the last straw of there croolty, which was: the small Yuman pikked up Fox 7, now ded, and flung him threw the air! Poor Fox 7, my frend, was spinning wile saling, like something long with a wate at one end! And what did those Yumans do? Stood bent over, laffing so hard! Then retreeved there crool hats and went bak to werk, slaping hands, as if what they had done was gud, and cul, and had made them glad.

Rest of the day I hid amung those dirt klods, kwietly wimpering.

When darkness fell I snuk over and vewed what remaned of Fox 7.

I had herd many Storys at that window but never had I herd a Story in which anything like what hapened to pore Fox 7 hapened. I did not know a Fox cud look that way. Even our Foxes who got hit by Kars did not look as bad as Fox 7.

And it was Yumans had done it.

I troted all nite, tray stunned. I wud stop to sleep, but dreem of Fox 7 and his sad last glanse. Kwaking there under the moon, I wud remember the nise way Fox 7 had of doing a nosenudge, if a frend of his mite be feeling low. Then I wud rise and run, trying to ferget.

And by morning was kwite lost.

For days I romed, lerning many things, such as: A rode can pass over a River. There is more than one Mawl. A tree can flote in a lake. Sometimes Yumans run in groops, waring yelow. Once on a sine is a picture of a Duk chopping down a tree, by using as his ax another Duk, who looks tray mad. Soon my pads are bludy. There is no fud. Sometimes I cud find a Grasshopper. Once I fownd a ded Berd, who had been ded so long he had bad hi gene. So I cud not eat him. I tryed but no way.

Perhaps, reeder, you have herd that frase called: It was the best of times, it was the werst of times? (It is from a buk. Once that Mother tried reeding that buk to her cubs. But it pruved boring, with too many werds. Therebuy her cubs began doing what Yung Yumans do when bord, which is, rolling around with fingers up nose, pinching there baby brother.)

All I cud think was, Fox 7 is ded, and it is all my fawlt. Why had I ever had that dum idea of entering the Mawl? Why was I born so weerd? Why cud I not be a simple Fox, having no day-dreems, speeking just Fox, obaying my Grate Leeder?

It was the werst of times, it was the werst of times.

And tell the truth, my hart went slite lee bad.

Troting thru a forest, I wud heer such things as Berds swoping down prasing all nature, and Mise saying it is a super day, and Cows in a nearby feeld going, O wow, isn't the werld grate and so farth, we are just reely luvving this super grass. That is how Animals are: kwite cheer full. But I was not like that now. And knew I wud not be like that again. Now their songs of luv seemed like the dopy chater Fox 7 and I had been saying to each other as we lay

all hapy between those Fake Rox in the Mawl, sharing are hope full plans of getting pants and glases and so farth, and inviting Yumans to are Den, serving them some froot if we have some, all that time watching those Yumans with such luv, not knowing what was coming next, like two little Babys, fast asleep in the middle of a horeable werld, who did not yet know how horeable it reely is.

Sometimes, troting on my bludy pads threw a Yuman zone, such as RiverWalkEstates, along such rodes as Hummingbird Way and Slow Stream Ave or even Melody Manner Passage, seeing so many grate Dens, with lites like indoor suns, and water shooting majik lee out of there grass at will, seeing that long line of Kars trot away so proud every morning full of Yumans, and the other splenders Yumans cud do, such as make grass short, such as cause flowrs to grow inside there Dens, I woslike: Why did the Curator do it so rong, making the groop with the gratest skils the meenest?

Then one day I came upon a Forest, the like of which I had never seen before, so deep and green and dark and grate-smelling it made those holes in my nose go super wide with sheer delite. O, the lite threw the Trees! The moving shadows when the wind wud blow! The millyun grate smells, such as water not far away! The wind in the hi part of the Trees, and sometimes a branch will crak!

All of the suden, I smelled Fox big-time. Then saw Foxes big-time. A hole other groop. Just like us. Only not. Compared to us they were (1) less skiny and had (2) no feer in eyes and (3) cotes of the pretiest red ever, a deep Fox lee red that made me ashamed of my own dul cote.

I told them my name and let them smell me, hoping they wud like me.

Which they did. They did smell me. They did like me. They tuk turns smelling and liking me.

I told them all that had be fallen me. They beleeved it about the Mawl. They did not beleev it about Fox 7. I cud tell. They looked at me funy. Then looked at each other funy.

Tell the truth, I wud not have beleeved me either if I had showed up and told me that.

Those Foxes were super nise. One came over all shy and out of her mowth dropped a froot at my paw. One dropped a gift of a part of a Berd. They showed me to a pond, where I drank so much they were slitely laffing.

And I woslike: There is no fud or gud water where I live.

One of them woslike: We kind of figgered.

Then, thanks to my habit of day-dreeming, I saw myself, in my brane, leeding my other Foxes to this paradice, one by one, threw Fox-ViewCommons. I wud show them the Gap. I wud show them the Fake Rox. If one was skared I wud say: Don't be skared. And make a joke. If one was slow I wud give a push from behind with an enkeraging snout. If one was looking around all freeked out, I wud calm lee go: Fokus, fokus. If one was old, such as are Grate Leeder, I wud carry him or her on my bak.

Soon, in my mind, we are all safe lee there. And my other Foxes, looking at me with shy-glanses upturned, are like: Fox 8, we cud not have been more rong. And they fan me with there fans.

I snapped out from that day-dream to find the New Foxes regarding me with kind lee smiles.

When I told them my day-dreem, they were like: Cul. Bring your frends here, we can all live

together very hapy. There is so much fud here it is like crazy.

Wud it be easy?

It wud not. It wud take Guts. But I have Guts. I once likked the tire of a Truk that was moving to see how it tasted, which the Groop teesed me about it, because hey Fox 8, why not wate until one found a Truk not moving, wud that not be easier?

Only too bad. If this was a buk, all it wud take is Guts, and I cud have done it. But no. It was reel life. For many weeks I tried to find my Old Foxes. My new frends even helped.

But no way.

We serched and serched but never fownd my frends, or even a trase of FoxViewCommons.

It is as if my beluvved Old Groop had fallen off the fase of Erth. (Gudby deer frends. I will not forgit you.)

So now I live here. I have fud. I have water. I have frends. One frend is Fox SmallNose/Alert+Funy. She is prety. She is nise. These new Foxes do there names somewhat difrent, having werds in there names. These werds tell what is note werthy about each Fox. Like one Fox is known as Fox Complanes Constantly/Yet Nise. One is known as Fox WhySoHefty? My frend Fox SmallNose/Alert+Funy has a small nose, plus is alert, plus is funy. Hense her name.

Sometimes she is like: You are not all here, Fox 8. Come alive. Be hapy.

Yesterday she woslike: You have a sad dark view.

And I woslike: So wud you.

She woslike: Well, I do not want are Babys having a mopy dad.

To which I woslike: Wait, are we having Babys?

And she spun arownd, and did a hop-and-yip.

Hearing that gave me paws. I did not want to be the kind of Dad who is so mad he just skowls, and hense his Babys are like: Ugh, Dad brings us down, he does not find life gud, but only sits mad in the Den wile us other Foxes stare up at the moonlite, nuzzling close, moving our tale areas bak and forth the way we Foxes do when glad. I wanted to be the kind of Dad who, yeers hense, when thinking of me, are Babys are like, gud old Dad, he was always there for us, showing us with the old snout-nudge what is fud and what is not.

So asked myself: What mite somewhat re-treev the old and hope full me? And replyed: Some ansers.

Which is why I am riting this leter to you Yumans.

I wud like to know what is rong with you peeple. How cud the same type of Animal who made that luv lee Mawl make Fox 7 look the way he looked that time I saw him? Wud a Yuman do something like that to another Yuman? I dowt it. Whenever I saw a Yuman, he or she was laffing wile smiling wile approching the Mawl. Sometimes one Kar mite hit another Kar and a Yuman mite be slite lee mad, but always, by the end, they are at least nise, and give each other the gift of a scrap of paper. Never onse did I see a Yuman hit another Yuman with a rok hat, stomp and kik that Yuman, then fling that Yuman, laffing when he or she came down in a puff of dirt with a sikening sound.

Maybe Yumans do that.

But I have not seen it.

I know life can be gud. Most lee it is gud. I have drank cleen cold water on a hot day, herd the soft bark of the one I luv, watched sno fall slow, making the wuds kwiet. But now all these happy sites and sounds seem like triks. Now it seems like the gud times are mere lee smoke that, upon blowing away, here is the reel life, which is: rok hats, kikking, stomping. Every minit with no kikking and stomping now seems like not a real minit. Do you get what I mean? It is like some frend who pre-veusly was nise suden lee says some crool thing and does this nip on your flank. Even

when he goes bak to being nise, you will never feel exact lee safe. And meenwile your other frends, who did not get nipped, are troting arownd with hapy smiles, going: Fox 8, why so glum?

Preveus to lerning we wud have Babys, I felt, about Yumans: I brake with you. If you see

me in the wuds, do not come neer. Stay in your awesum howses, play your music lowd, however you make it play so lowd, yap your Yuman jokes, sending forth your crood laffter into the nite. I will not approche you. I will just stay in my plase, skwatting low, fearful and kwaking, which is how you seem to like us Foxes.

But now, Babys on root, I do not want to feel that way.

I want to feel strong and generus. I want to feel hope full. Which is why, upon compleeshun of this leter, I will leeve it at that howse at the end of Clear Circle Way, where offen I see a serten rownd guy feeding Berds. His male boks says his name is P. Melonsky. You seem nise enough, P. Melonsky. Reed my leter, go farth, ask your felow Yumans what is up, rite bak, leeve your anser under your Berd feeder, I will come in the nite to retreeve and lern.

I am sure there is some eksplanashun.

And wud luv to know it.

Reeding my Story bak just now, I woslike: O no, my Story is a bumer. There is the deth of a gud pal, and no plase of up lift, or lerning a leson. The nise Fox's first Groop stays lost, his frend stays ded.

Bla.

If you Yumans wud take one bit of advise

from a meer Fox? By now I know that you Yu-mans like your Storys to end hapy?

If you want your Storys to end happy, try being niser.

I awate your answer.

Fox 8

ABOUT THE AUTHOR

GEORGE SAUNDERS is the author of ten books, including *Tenth of December*, which was a finalist for the National Book Award and won the inaugural Folio Prize (for the best work of fiction in English) and the Story Prize (best short-story collection). He has received MacArthur and Guggenheim fellowships and the PEN/Malamud Prize for excellence in the short story, and was recently elected to the American Academy of Arts and Sciences. In 2013, he was named one of the world's 100 most influential people by *Time* magazine. His novel, *Lincoln in the Bardo,* debuted at #1 on the *New York Times* bestseller list, and won the 2017 Man Booker Prize. He teaches in the creative writing program at Syracuse University.

georgesaundersbooks.com
Facebook.com/GeorgeSaundersFans

ABOUT THE ILLUSTRATOR

CHELSEA CARDINAL is an artist working across various mediums of design, illustration, and fashion. She grew up on the Canadian prairies and now lives in Brooklyn. In her next life, if it is up to her, she would like to be a fox.

chelseacardinal.com
Instagram: @chelseacardinal

ABOUT THE TYPE

This book was set in Nofret, a typeface designed in 1986 by Gudrun Zapf-von Hesse especially for the Berthold foundry.